Hurry Up, Pony!

First published in 2008
by Wayland

This paperback edition published in 2009 by Wayland

Text copyright © Jillian Powell 2008
Illustration copyright © Stefania Colnaghi 2008

Wayland
338 Euston Road
London NW1 3BH

Wayland Australia
Hachette Children's Books
Level 17/207 Kent Street
Sydney, NSW 2000

The rights of Jillian Powell to be identified as the Author
and Stefania Colnaghi to be identified as the Illustrator of this Work have
been asserted by them in accordance with the Copyright, Designs and
Patents Act, 1988.

Series Editor: Louise John
Editor: Katie Powell
Cover design: Paul Cherrill
Design: D.R.ink
Consultant: Shirley Bickler

A CIP catalogue record for this book is available from the British Library.

ISBN 9780750252188 (hbk)
ISBN 9780750252195 (pbk)

Printed in China

Wayland is a division of Hachette Children's Books,
an Hachette Livre UK Company
www.hachettelivre.co.uk

Hurry Up, Pony!

Written by Jillian Powell
Illustrated by Stefania Colnaghi

WAYLAND

Rosie went for a pony ride.

The pony stopped
to eat the grass.

"Off we go!" Rosie said.

They saw Megan so the
pony stopped for a pat.

"Let's go now!" Rosie said.

They saw a scarecrow and the pony stopped for a look.

"Walk on!" Rosie said.

Then they saw Dad.

The pony stopped
for an apple.

"Time to go!" Rosie said.

They went up a hill.
The pony stopped
for a rest.

"Trot on!" Rosie said.

Then the pony stopped
for a drink.

"Hurry up!" Rosie said.

The pony saw a tractor and stopped again.

The pony saw carrots in the back of the tractor.

START READING is a series of highly enjoyable books for beginner readers. They have been carefully graded to match the Book Bands widely used in schools. This enables readers to be sure they choose books that match their own reading ability.

The Bands are:

| Pink / Band 1 |
| Red / Band 2 |
| Yellow / Band 3 |
| Blue / Band 4 |
| Green / Band 5 |
| Orange / Band 6 |
| Turquoise / Band 7 |
| Purple / Band 8 |
| Gold / Band 9 |

START READING books can be read independently or shared with an adult. They promote the enjoyment of reading through satisfying stories supported by fun illustrations.

Jillian Powell started writing stories when she was four years old. She has written many books for children, including stories about cats, dogs, scarecrows and ghosts.

Stefania Colnaghi lives with her husband in a small village near Pavia, in northern Italy. She loves drawing animals and naughty children and in her free time enjoys walking in the hills around her home with her dogs.